LEVI, THE LITTLE SHEPHERD BOY

Levi, The Little Shepherd Boy

Steve Brown
The Artist: Kyria Beals
Edited by: Krista Hill, L Talbott

ELM HILL

A Division of
HarperCollins Christian Publishing

www.elmhillbooks.com

Published in Nashville, Tennessee, by Elm Hill, an imprint of Thomas Nelson. Elm Hill and Thomas Nelson are registered trademarks of HarperCollins Christian Publishing, Inc.

Elm Hill titles may be purchased in bulk for educational, business, fund-raising, or sales promotional use. For information, please e-mail SpecialMarkets@ ThomasNelson.com.

Publisher's Note: This novel is a work of fiction. Names, characters, places, and incidents are either products of the author's imagination or used fictitiously. All characters are fictional, and any similarity to people living or dead is purely coincidental.

Library of Congress Cataloging-in-Publication Data

Library of Congress Control Number: 2019912366

ISBN 978-1-400328840 (Paperback)
ISBN 978-1-400328857 (Hardbound)
ISBN 978-1-400328864 (eBook)

My name is Levi. I am a shepherd, like all the men in my family before me. Since my childhood I have tended sheep which—except for an occasional wolf, lion, or thief threatening the flock—is an uneventful job.

That is, but for one unforgettable event that happened many years ago, when I was a boy.

I, along with my brothers, used to watch our sheep as they roamed and grazed on the hillsides just outside the small town of Bethlehem, in the kingdom of Judah. We would be stuck out in the wilderness for weeks. Water was sometimes in short supply, so bathing wasn't always an option—and boy did we smell!

I would spend my days looking out over the flock, but not always watching the sheep. I was lost in my daydreams.... I dreamt of owning my own vineyard, where I could grow fine grapes and not have to watch smelly sheep all day! I hoped for the time when I would not have my older brothers telling me what to do!

My brothers always teased me because of my size: I was small for my age. "Little shepherd boy!" they would call me as they pushed me around. They would make fun of me for being weak and frail, and soon I became bitter and resentful. I didn't feel like I fit in at all.

One night my brothers sent me off alone to watch the sheep while they sat around the campfire and told their stories. "King David was a shepherd boy like you," they said. "Go watch the sheep like King David!"

10

I grumbled as I headed for my favorite spot on the hillside. As I walked along, the sky became unusually bright. I looked up and saw the most brilliant light I had ever seen.

As I marveled at the magnificent star, angels suddenly appeared in the heavens. One of them spoke out: "Do not be afraid! I bring you a message of great importance and joy for all people! A Savior has been born in Bethlehem, the City of David. He is Christ the Lord and you will find him in a manger, wrapped in swaddling clothes!"

The angels began to say, "Glory to God in the highest!" The sounds of their ringing voices echoed across the land. All at once I had feelings of peace, comfort, and belonging.

I raced back to the campfire to tell my brothers what I had seen. When I arrived, they were all gathering their things. I heard my oldest brother say they were going to Bethlehem to see the babe in the manger.

"Wait for me!" I cried.

"What?" my brother said. "You must stay here and tend the sheep! Get back to the flock before a wolf comes!"

"But, I heard the angel speak!" I said.

All my brothers laughed and began to taunt me.

"Why would an angel speak to a small boy like you?...

You are of no importance...Go back to the sheep!"

They all walked off toward Bethlehem, leaving me standing there, alone. I became angry as I kicked a rock across the ground and shook my fist. "Enough!" I cried. I would leave it all: my family, the sheep, all of it! I was tired of being the smallest, the weakest, the least important. I would go out into the world and I would show all of them someday!

I ran off, not knowing where I was going.

I only knew I wanted to be far away. As I looked in the direction of Bethlehem, I saw the huge and wondrous star in the sky, its light beaming down on the stables outside the town. I became curious and followed the star.

When I arrived, I saw my brothers, along with many other shepherds as well as townsfolk, all gathered around a small stable. I pushed my way through the crowd until I could see what they were looking at: it was a baby! He lay in a manger as people prayed and spoke with excited voices: "The Savior from the House of David has come!"

I frowned as I looked at the little baby. He didn't look all that important as he lay atop the small mound of hay. He turned his head toward me and our eyes met. All at once, I felt a warm and peaceful light enter my soul. I no longer wanted to run away. I was no longer mad at my family. I wasn't even mad at the sheep!

The sheep!

I raced back toward the sheep as quickly as I could, hoping that no wolves, lions, or thieves had come for them. Along the way, I saw my brothers. I stopped and waited for them to yell at me for abandoning the flock, but instead, they all hugged me and said they forgave me!

"God will protect the sheep," my oldest brother said, "while we are together as a family."

That night, I gave God my life, all because of his son, Jesus—the baby who lay in the manger. If God can change the hearts of poor shepherds, just think what he can do for all the hearts in the world!

After all these many years, I remember that night as I watch over my sheep. My vineyard dreams are long forgotten. I am content to be who I am. As I roam the hills and watch over my flock, I no longer need a star in the sky, for the light of God shines from within my heart…

And He could be in your heart, too!

CPSIA information can be obtained
at www.ICGtesting.com
Printed in the USA
LVHW072124131119
637306LV00015B/57/P